HIDe

Tabitha Leigh

The Bookish Berg

The Bookish Berg

ISBN: 979-8-9905149-6-6

For my brother, Steve.
WOLVERINES!

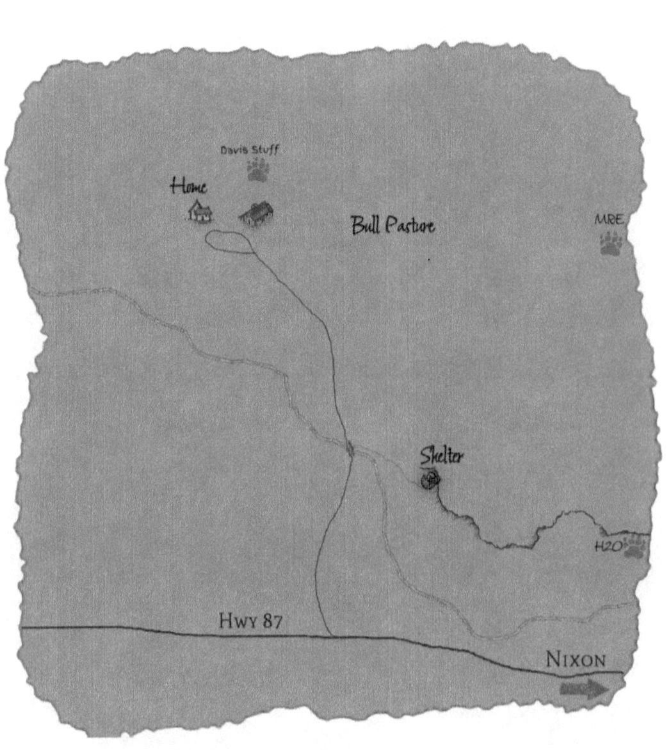

Davis Stuff
Home
Bull Pasture
M.R.E.
Shelter
H2O
Hwy 87
Nixon

December 2nd, 2023

Cade's breath was coming hard and fast, tearing at his lungs like knives. He pumped his legs with all the strength he had up the long, winding road. The pecan trees lining the drive had dropped their bounty, and the brittle shells scattered as he charged through. He grunted with the strain as he sprinted the last few yards to his family's home. Just as he bounded over the metal cattle guard, he heard Tara scream.

"Cade! No!"

Her voice cut past the raw emotion pouring through his brain. It was enough for him to skid to a halt, reality crashing back. As much as he wanted to charge into the house, he knew he couldn't. The battle of the century raged inside his heart as he yearned to run to his mother's rescue.

She was just inside the door.

She was probably on the couch, smelling like gardenias and fresh bread.

She needed him, and he didn't dare go near.

A primal sound welled in his belly as he sobbed and fell to the ground, clutching at the gravel with his fists.

After a few minutes, his head cleared enough to slow his breathing. He heard the soft crunching of gravel behind him, and then Tara was there, sliding her arm around his trembling shoulders. With gentle pressure, she guided him to stand, mindful of blocking his view of the house as she turned him away toward the road.

"We need to get back to the kids."

Together, they walked and stumbled back down the road to the creek, where they silently turned and made their way to the shelter.

The shelter had begun as a childhood obsession. Cade and Tara had both discovered each other in the library over a book about zombies. She had checked it out and had never returned it, and he had been waiting for the book - too long, he had thought. He sweet-talked the librarian, Mrs. Moody, into telling him who had the book, and in the end, he had every intention of retrieving it. That first knock on Tara's front door never produced the book, but it did begin a friendship and a mission that ran deep.

Planning for a zombie apocalypse started as the two of them chasing good stories, but it culminated in preparations and planning to rival a large-scale emergency management operation.

Just before they crawled through the tangled morning glory vines, Cade paused. Tara, who had been leading the way, turned.

"I would have done the same thing, y'know."

Her expression was no-nonsense as usual - she was never one for embellishment.

Cade could do little more than glare at the dirt. A long minute passed, and then he finally spoke.

"She's gone, isn't she?"

Tara studied him for a moment. Her reddish hair was twisted up in a messy knot, and she wore no make-up. Her grey tank top and jeans were standard Tara - the 22 caliber rifle slung across her back was the only difference. She narrowed her eyes and looked hard at Cade.

"You knew the answer to that before you took off. They're all dead. And if they aren't, they will be before long."

Without another word, she turned and disappeared through the hanging morning glory vines, leaving them swaying gently in the silence that followed.

CHAPTER 1

Attack - December 2, 2023

"Cade!"

Debbie Stevens voice carried up the stairs. Cade groaned and rolled out of bed. He felt around under his bed for his jeans and pulled them on. He was still rubbing the sleep out of his eyes as his bedroom door burst open.

"Hey!" he yelled at the intruder. His older brother Dylan laughed and launched a balled-up sweatshirt at his head. Cade swatted it away and made a leap at the door. Dylan met his attack and the two tumbled onto Cade's bed rolling and faking punches and swats.

"Boys!"

Their mother appeared in the doorway, laughing.

"I swear you still act like you did ten years ago!" She leaned over, picked up the sweatshirt and tossed it back to Cade.

"Get dressed. Dylan is going to drive you in to school on his way out of town."

"Yeah, stinky, get dressed or I'm leaving your butt!" Dylan laughed and strode out of the room. Cade saw Davis run past his door after their older brother.

"Dylan, wait!!"

Cade finished dressing and pulled on his sneakers. He grabbed his backpack and headed downstairs where the smell of breakfast made his mouth water. He was reaching for the bacon when his father's voice boomed from the front room.

"Boys! Better hit the road."

Stuffing a piece of bacon into his mouth, Cade trailed behind Dylan through the kitchen door and down the hallway to the front of the house.

William Stevens was standing in the living room at the big bay windows, his arms crossed in front as he surveyed the sky.

"Looks like that weather is gonna get here quicker than ol' Steve Browne thought." As both boys entered the room, he turned. His stern face rarely showed amusement, but he offered a small smile and gave his oldest son a quick handshake.

"You take care now, boy. We'll see you in a month or so when we head up your direction."

Dylan nodded.

"Yessir. Will do." He hefted his duffle bag and opened the front door, waiting for Cade to follow.

"Ya'll go on now. Git!"

Mr. Stevens ushered the boys out the door and closed it behind them. Cade and Dylan trotted down the front porch steps toward Dylan's 84 Ford F150. Dylan tossed the bag behind the seat and climbed in while Cade took another look at the gathering clouds on the horizon.

"C'mon little brother! Let's roll!"

Cade climbed in, shut he door and the engine roared to life. The truck skidded on the gravel as Dylan punched the gas. They boys were down the gravel road, turning onto the interstate when the first drops of rain spattered the windshield. Dylan turned the wipers on as the rain turned from a sprinkle to a downpour.

"You gonna be ok?" Dylan was looking at his younger brother.

"Yeah, why wouldn't I?"

"You just look a little tense."

Cade looked out the window then back at his brother.

"It's all good," he lied.

"Man," Dylan started, "you are a *terrible* liar." He chuckled. "Really, dude. What's going on?"

Cade shook his head, "It's nothing, really!"

"Look, if it's coach crawling up your a-"

"It's not that." Cade cut him off.

Dylan stared ahead at the road. He gripped the steering wheel a little tighter and said, "'It's because I am leaving."

Cade winced. He didn't want his brother to think of him as weak, and it was taking everything he had not to cry. He shifted in his seat uncomfortably.

"Man, this is going to be a great thing. My college will be paid for so mom and dad can focus on the ranch. I'll get to go all over the world and," he glanced over at his brother, "you can come visit me wherever I am. Germany, Japan, you name it!" Dylan smiled and put on his best salesman face.

The truck was pulling up to the high school and kids were straggling in. Dylan took a turn in the parking lot and pulled up to the curb outside to gym and locker rooms. Cade grabbed the door handle and pulled. As he stepped out of the truck, he looked back at his brother.

"Look, just take care of yourself and come home, ok?"

"Dude, this is basic training. Not Afghanistan." Dylan chuckled and shook his head. "Get out of here, you nerd!"

Cade smiled back and stepped away from the track as he closed the passenger door. His brother waved and pulled away. Cade stood in the rain, watching as his brother's truck turned out of the lot and sped away. Slowly, he turned back towards the gym and made his way to the double doors.

"Cade!"

He turned to find his best friend Tara sprinting from the parking lot. Her expression was disgruntled - her usual demeanor. They both ducked under the awning at the gym doors.

"Shoot me. Now," she grumbled as they found an empty space on the bleachers. Tara hurled her backpack into the wooden stands, flopping unceremoniously onto the bench.

"Um, ok. Let me unpack the rifle I usually carry to school." Cade shook his head and smirked. Tara shot him a mean glare.

"What did your mom do?"

Tara's mom desperately wanted her only daughter to be like the other girls in their small Texas town. She had signed her up for twirling lessons when she was seven and dance and gymnastics at eight, and when those didn't work, she entered her in the Little Miss Gonzales County pageant. Tara had a meltdown, but her mom was persistent.

"I have to babysit. BABYSIT!" She paused, then sighed. "And it's little girls. Ugh!"

"Who?"

"Brianna and Allison from next door. You know, the Rainbow Wing freaks?"

"Hey, it's not that bad. Maybe you can un-girl them!" Cade tried not to laugh, but his amusement was impossible to hide.

"Well, I will do my best. I have to sort through the new box of MRE's. I think I will give them a crash course on prepping." Tara checked her phone and then reached to grab her backpack. Tossing it over her shoulder, she stood and headed for the door. "See you at lunch!" she called out over her shoulder as she disappeared out the door.

CHAPTER 2

Into the Brush

THE REST OF THE school day was uneventful. The best part of his day was lunch and computer science - mostly because he loved working in the lab and both classes were with Tara. When the bell rang at the end of class, they walked out of school together. Tara stopped at the front sidewalk and started toward the other side of the school complex.

"I'll be right back. I have to grab the girls over at the elementary. They have to come home with me," she called over her shoulder.

Cade nodded and sat on the low rock wall outside the front of the high school main building to wait for his little brother. Davis had soccer at the end of the day, so he usually came from the gym and met Cade out in front. Their mother picked him, Tara, and Davis up after football practice, but because the practice had been canceled while the field was under construction, the kids had the lucky reprieve from after-school activities. This whole week Cade and Tara had been working on their shelter and preparing more printed resources. He had to ensure Mom stopped in Cuero at the Walmart to grab more ink for his printer. She was supposed to go on a grocery run today, and he hoped she hadn't forgotten.

Ten minutes later Cade was joined by Davis, sweaty and loud as usual. He came running out of the gym and all but tackled Cade.

"Incoming!"

"Cut it out!" Cade pushed his brother back and tried to sit back up on the wall.

"God. I was just playing." Davis settled into a pout until a group of his friends walked by. His face brightened back up and he sprinted to catch up with them. As Davis took off, Tara and her new charges walked up from the other side of the school grounds. Tara looked completely disgusted, with two younger girls dressed in pink and purple trailing behind her. The scene was comical, almost to the point of hilariousness. Tara plopped down beside Cade and told the girls to stand beside her.

"Do you think your mom will mind dropping the girls and I by my house on the way out?"

"Nah, probably not. You're just off the highway anyway."

"Where's Davis?"

Cade scanned the area in front of the gym for his brother but saw no one. Over in the parking lot he noticed more parents were pulling in to pick up their kids – more than usual. He glanced at his watch. Three forty-five. His mom was usually earlier. At that moment, he heard squealing tires and a horn honking. He turned to see his mother come tearing into the side administration lot. Her haphazardness took Cade by surprise. Before he could stand up, she had rolled the window down.

"Cade! Where's your brother?"

She was shouting. Cade, flustered by his mother's behavior, looked wildly around for Davis. He was nowhere to be seen. A flash of neon green came into view at the edge of the gym building. There!

"Davis!" Cade yelled. His brother stepped out from behind the gym looking toward van's direction with a strange expression.

Cade's mother was outside the van, hollering directly at her youngest son.

"Davis Miller Stevens! Let's go! Now!"

Without even asking, Cade opened the van's side door and motioned for the girls to get in.

"Mom, we have to take Tara by her house on the way out." Cade climbed into the front passenger seat as Davis jumped in behind the girls and slammed the door shut.

"No time."

Mrs. Stevens was already back in and throwing it into gear. Cade stared at his mother, unable to process her behavior. She reached over and flipped on the radio.

" – at this time. Unconfirmed reports seem to indicate the virus is being spread through the air."

Cade snapped the radio off.

"What's going on mom?" Davis was practically climbing over into the front seats.

"Sit down!" she shouted.

The whole van fell into complete silence. Mrs. Stevens took a deep breath and gripped the wheel.

"There's something going on. People are dy-" she looked in the rear-view mirror at the two young girls in the back seat. "um, getting very sick. The radio is saying it's in the air. Maybe the water."

"You mean like the anthrax thing a long time ago?" Tara looked a little too excited.

"Yes, but worse. No one knows what it is, but it is showing up everywhere. All over the country." Mrs. Stevens flipped open her phone and dialed. "Not every news station has picked up on it yet."

"Who would do this?" Cade muttered to himself.

"C'mon, Bill. Pick up!" She waited a few more seconds then snapped it closed and tossed it onto the dash. She looked at Cade.

"What?"

"Who's doing this?" he repeated.

"So far, no one has claimed it. But I'm willing to bet it's a terrorist thing." Cade's mom reached back over and turned the radio back on. She raised her arm and with one motion, silenced the van.

" - reports have been coming in from all over the country. Officials have been combing through flight logs and airport records hoping to find some correlation. We have a few, new similar reports of a yellowish substance in the water in New York City and in same areas of Colorado and Texas. Scientists at the CDC are working to identify the substance. We will stay with you until we have further information."

"Mom?"

Cade could only stare at his mother while she drove in silence. The car stayed quiet until they got to the gravel road that led up to the house. She stopped the van just as they turned off the highway and then turned to look at everyone.

"I am going to drop you all off at the creek. I want you to go to your playhouse-"

"Shelter," Cade cut in. His mother frowned.

"Okay, shelter, and stay there until I come for you. Cade, Tara, I know you have some supplies there, so you should be okay while I'm gone."

"Mom-" Davis started.

"No talking. Just do as I say." She turned to Cade. "There's a .22 in the back. I'll drop ammo by after I go to the house."

She had begun to speak rapidly and then pause for a moment, seeming to try and collect herself. She took a deep breath and asked, "Do you have enough water stashed up there?"

Cade couldn't think. He couldn't process anything. He had gone blank. His mother looked to Tara.

"Tara, do you guys have water out there?"

"Yes, ma'am."

"What about food and blankets? Batteries?"

"Mrs. Stevens, we have everything. We'll be good."

"Mom, what are you going to do?" Davis called out from the seat behind her.

"I am going back to the house and get some things for you. Then I'm going to get your dad from Luling. Everyone in town knows we have guns and other such stuff. We'll be back in a day or two, then he and I can head out to join you till things settle down."

Davis flung himself over her seat and grabbed her in an embrace.

"No, mom! I'm coming with you."

She pushed him back to look at him closely. "Davis, I need you to help your brother. You have some extra company that needs looking after and you are an important part of the team." She stroked his hair tenderly and smiled.

"I will be fine. But I won't be okay if I have to worry about you. You get your things and go with Cade." With that she grabbed him close again and hugged him hard. She looked at Cade.

"You know what to do. What your dad and I taught you." She gave Cade a weak smile.

He nodded, his resolve building.

She released Davis and turned back to the steering wheel, tapping the gas and creeping forward down the road. About three minutes later, they arrived at the old concrete bridge spanning the creek where Mrs. Stevens stopped and opposed open the rear door. When Cade made his way back to her, he was surprised to see bags of dry goods, several packages of toilet paper, and a sack filled with what looked like first aid supplies. She stuck her hands down underneath the stash and pulled out the rifle and handed it to Cade.

"I was stocking up for our Christmas vacation at the cabin. Good thing, hm?" she said, nodding to the assortment of plastic bags. She called out to all the children.

"Kids! Empty out your backpacks and start stuffing them with what I have back here. Hurry!" She kept looking over her shoulder.

Tara, Cade and Davis immediately did as she asked and started stuffing everything they could into their bags. Allison and Brianna simply stood there, tears streaming down their faces. In the rush, the two girls had been afterthoughts.

Debbie Stevens knelt down and gathered the girls up in a hug. When she was satisfied the girls felt a little better, she looked at them both.

"Girls, Cade and Tara are going to take you camping. I am going to call your mom and dad to make sure it's ok. If they want you to come home later this evening, I will take you, Ok?" She waited for them to respond. Allison, the oldest spoke first.

"Dad is out of town. But my mom said she would be back home by eight o'clock."

"Well, good then! You'll have time to enjoy yourself in case you have to leave tonight. Now, help the others load up the camping supplies, ok?"

Cade stopped briefly and stared at his mother. He could not imagine how or where she got the strength not to panic. She sounded like a regular mom - like nothing much was happening. It was amazing and he loved her for it.

The girls nodded and began hesitantly filling their matching Hello Kitty backpacks with toilet paper and band-aids. Once the backpacks were stuffed, Cade's mother gave each of them a quick embrace and motioned for them to go. Cade was last. She stopped him as the others began to follow Tara into the brush.

"Do not come to the house. You hear me? Don't even think about it. I don't know what's going on or if I am overreacting, but you are too important to me to risk. Stay put and listen to the radio. If I need you, I will come to you. That's it. Don't come to the house, you hear?"

Cade had begun to tremble. His adrenaline had kicked in. He looked at his mother who appeared so fierce. She was expecting him to take care of Tara and Davis and the Holder girls. He thought he could do it – maybe. She pulled him into an embrace.

Just before his mother pulled away, he gripped her close. Trying to disguise the tears that threatened to fall, he whispered, "Those two old surplus gas masks of Uncle Miller's are in my room. In the bottom left drawer of my desk. Get them. For you and Dad."

His mother nodded and pulled away, wiping tears out of her own eyes.

"Ok, son. Go!" his mother hugged him hard one last time, then she was running around the driver's side of the van. Within seconds, the van was gone up the gravel road leaving a trail of dust. Cade lingered for a moment, then he turned and started climbing up the trail through the brush.

CHAPTER 3

Taking Stock

THE FIRST ONE TO notice him was Davis, who ran to him and hugged him tightly. The enormity of the past hour hit him in the chest in the form of his brother, and Cade clutched him tightly. He heard Tara gather the girls and usher them into the cave entrance. Davis was shuddering, probably crying. Cade pressed his face into his brother's hair.

"Aw, buddy. It's okay."

Davis sniffled and pulled back, looking up at Cade. The streaks down his face were layered - he'd been crying a lot today. Cade knelt in front of his little brother and looked him in the eye.

"You've got me. I'm not leaving your side. You hear me?" Cade waited for his words to soak in. Davis looked at the ground and nodded his head almost imperceptibly. The nine-year-old, who had always been a wild-eyed force of nature, suddenly seemed so fragile and small. Davis had always been naturally loud and boisterous and full of life with a wicked sense of humor and a hot temper as well. Now, he seemed to pull inside himself.

"Hey, Tank. Did you hear me?"

Davis looked up at Cade's use of his family nickname. The slightest hint of relief showed around his eyes, and he fell forward again into his brother's arms. Cade felt him murmur something against his neck, but he didn't bother to ask him to repeat it. He imagined the words were "I love you." It was enough to give him resolve, so he stood and took Davis by the shoulders. "Let's go in and get this figured out, okay?"

The two boys entered the shelter and sat down around Tara's small fire in the pit near the front. Along the shelter's inner walls, rows of large plastic bins were stacked two deep, and a pile of coats and blankets overflowed out of a cracked plastic garbage can. The floor was hard-packed dirt, and most of the ceiling was smooth, river-worn limestone. Here and there, clumps of dirt with stray weeds filled holes in the cement and rock walls., but the little green wisps of grass were turning brown and brittle at their ends.

The mood was somber. Tara took a breath to speak, then hesitated as she glanced at Cade. He nodded to her.

"Okay, everyone. Here's the deal. We're gonna be here for a little while," she started. She continued, "But that's okay because we have plenty of supplies."

"What do you mean we are going to be here a while? What's really going on?" Allison demanded. She stood up and crossed her arms in front of her. "I want you to take me home. My mom wouldn't like this!"

Tara looked uncertain.

"Allison," Cade put his hands up. "We don't know what's going on." He squatted in front of Allison, until he was at eye level with her. "But you can bet if my mom said to come up here and stay put, that's what we should do. She wouldn't do anything to make your mom mad, and actually, I think your mom would be happy that you girls were safe."

Allison still looked skeptical.

"You know," Tara joined in, "I'm your babysitter, so I'm in charge of you. I say it's okay for you to be here," Tara tried to look reassuring.

"And when my mom calls your mom, if it's not okay, she'll come and get you like she said," Cade smiled at Allison, who offered him a weak expression of trust.

Brianna, who had remained silent, looked at everyone with a sad expression.

"I'm scared."

It was barely more than a whisper.

Cade sat beside her and folded her up in his arms.

"Me, too kiddo," he said. "But I know I will take care of you for your mom until you get back to her. We all will."

CHAPTER 4

What's Going On Out There?

"WHAT WILL WE EAT?" Brianna's voice was small.

This time, Davis spoke up.

"Look around! There's food everywhere." He picked up a can of green beans and a package of juice boxes. He tossed one to Brianna, who didn't move to catch it.

"How do we know it's okay?" She stared at the brightly colored container on the dirt floor.

"Our stuff's okay, sweetie," Tara said. She picked the juice up and gave it to the younger girl. "We've been stashing this stuff for a long time. Way before any of this started."

Cade stood and leaned over Bri to get a bottle of water. He twisted the cap and added, "And there's more that we can get."

Tara continued, "One of us can go to the other place we stored supplies if the time comes that we need them." She smiled, a rare break from her usually serious demeanor.

"Okay, ladies," Cade stood and brushed his hands on his jeans. "Let's get ourselves situated. We've got another hour or so before it gets dark. We need to get ready for tonight."

"I'll get set up in here." Tara began rummaging through the pile of blankets and old sleeping bags. Cade remembered when they started hauling them to this place about a year ago. She could barely carry one all the way, and now she could haul two or three with no problem. She was a very determined and capable person. It was the reason he started talking to her in the first place.

"Tara, will you look for the radio? I'll need to check around outside to be sure no critters decided to call this place home. I don't want a skunk surprising us in the middle of the night."

"I will," she said without turning around.

Cade ducked outside and began picking his way around the area in front of their little shelter. It wasn't quite a cave, but rather a deep cut-in where the creek used to flow. He and Tara hauled large rocks up to the wall in the exposed opening, using a couple of "borrowed" bags of dry cement. He smiled, remembering their arguments about where to put the entrance. It was a good shelter, complete with an opening for their fire. On either side, a steep, rocky incline lead up to more pasture land.

The memories of the two of them working together out here brought a smile to his lips, but the yip of distant coyotes brought him back to reality, and he couldn't help but stop every couple of minutes to listen for the sound of tires on the road or the horn of his mom's van.

Cade finished checking the area just as Tara emerged, her phone in her hand. She looked visibly worried.

"What is it?"

"There's no signal." She held up her phone for him to see the bars fluctuate from one to no bars.

"How's that?" he murmured, taking the phone from her. The bars continued to fluctuate erratically. He looked up at Tara.

"You don't ever have signal problems out here, do you?" he asked.

"No. It never even switches to roam unless I take it past Stockdale, and then it's only sometimes, depending on the weather."

He pushed past her and entered the cave, making a beeline for his backpack. He dug through the outside pocket and fished out his phone. He pushed the power button, but the phone didn't turn on. He had forgotten to charge it, as usual.

"Tara!" he called.

"Yeah?"

"Where's the radio?"

She came inside, shaking her head.

"I was going to tell you before you ran back in here that it's dead. The batteries are toast."

CHAPTER 5

Hunkering Down

"DIDN'T WE STORE MORE batteries?"

Davis started to dig through all the storage containers. He pulled out a plastic grocery bag filled with packages of batteries. "What size?" he called out.

"D, I think," Tara said as she went over and sat down next to Davis. She rummaged through the bag, then triumphantly pulled out a sealed package of four D batteries. "Score!"

The batteries were in the radio within minutes, and Tara switched it to "ON." All five kids held their breath. Nothing. Tara turned the dial in both directions, but there was nothing. She threw her hands up in exasperation. "Now what?"

The sun was setting, and the temperature was falling. It was going to get chilly.

"I'll go grab some wood to keep this fire going; then we're going to eat and get some rest." Cade stood up and motioned to Tara. "Wanna give me a hand?"

She nodded as she stood and followed Cade outside. Once they were several feet away from the shelter, he turned.

"If mom hasn't come by morning, I'm going to check on her."

"Cade! You heard her. She said to stay put." Tara picked up a large branch at her feet and snapped it into two pieces. They walked in silence for a minute or two, gathering what wood they could see by the moonlight that had emerged. Finally, Cade spoke.

"I know she would be mad. But this waiting around for her is killing me!"

Tara stared at him for a moment.

"At least you know where your mother is. At least you have some idea about what is happening with your family!" Her eyes were welling with tears.

Cade drew in a breath.

"Tara, I'm sorry. I didn't mean to sound selfish." He dropped his bundle of wood, grabbed his best friend, and pulled her into a bear hug. She rested her head on his shoulder momentarily, then pulled back, rubbing her sniffling nose.

"Okay. Enough whining. We prepared for this kind of thing, so let's at least act like we know what we're doing."

Cade smiled and bent to pick up the wood he dropped, and the two returned to the shelter. Tara and the girls busied themselves with setting up sleeping bags and blankets while Cade and Davis banked the fire and pulled out food for dinner. When everything was set, they all gathered around the warmth of the fire and ate a quiet dinner of peanut butter crackers, fruit punch, and beef jerky.

As Tara was tucking the girls into their sleeping bags, Brianna asked, "When's my mommy coming?"

"I don't know," Tara frowned, then her expression brightened. "You get some sleep. and when someone comes, I'll wake you up. Dreaming is better than just sitting here bored out of your mind, right?"

Brianna nodded and tucked her hands under her chin while Allison wiggled closer to her sister. Cade glanced at Davis, who was fiddling with the radio. "Hey, little man," he called softly.

Davis looked up.

"Time to hit the sack." Cade patted the sleeping bag next to him.

Davis reluctantly laid the radio on a storage bin and crawled beside Cade. He lay down atop the flannel bag and looked at his big brother. Though he tried to disguise it, Cade could see the worry in his eyes. He put a hand on Davis' arm.

"Everything's gonna be okay, you know," he said, trying to sound reassuring.

Davis nodded.

"I know. I am just worried about mom and dad."

"Don't you worry about mom. She's smart. And tough. Even dad is afraid of her!"

Davis chuckled, then pulled his legs up to tuck them under the blanket. Cade pulled the sleeping bag over his younger brother's shoulders, then ruffled his hair.

"G'night, Tank."

"Night, Cade."

Cade stood, grabbing the rifle and slinging it over his shoulder. Tara looked up.

"Where are you going?"

"I'm taking the first watch. Get some sleep. I'll wake you in about four hours."

Cade turned and quietly stepped outside the shelter while Tara finished putting the jerky packets away. He lingered by the entrance and heard her slip into her sleeping bag. Wrapping his arms around himself, he closed his eyes momentarily and prayed for the world to be back to normal when he woke her up.

CHAPTER 6

Rinse, Repeat

"CADE."

Someone was shaking him.

"Cade, get up. Your turn."

He opened his eyes to find Davis looking at him. The moon was high, and the fire had all but died. Davis looked sleepy but seemed more confident now that he had completed a night watch. Cade groggily sat up. He never intended to fall asleep but must have been more worn out than he realized. He smiled at his brother.

"Good job, buddy." He rolled up to his knees and reached for the rifle Davis held in his hands. Davis handed it to him and yawned.

"Go lay down. Get some sleep, okay?"

Davis nodded and stepped over Tara to his bedroll. His eyes were closed before his head hit the pillow made of old coats. Cade smiled to himself. They all had to grow up much more quickly in the space of the last few days than anyone ever should. Cade and Davis were in limbo, not knowing about their parents and their older brother. They had begun to assume the worst since their parents had not yet come for them, while Tara had no idea about her mother. The girls were in the same boat. In this shelter Cade and Tara put together to withstand a so-called zombie apocalypse, the kids were safe but isolated from the world. Davis fixed the radio, but they were afraid to listen for fear of what they would hear. Mostly, they held their breath, waiting to hear the honk of the van down by the creek, but it hadn't come yet. Cade was beginning to believe it never would.

He ducked out of the cave and made his way to the big, old oak. Tonight, he decided to climb up to the fork in the trunk and see if he could make out lights in the town. If there were still people there, it might mean everything was okay, and they could turn on the radio to hear what was going on in the world.

The breeze was a little more than chilly but not bone-crushingly cold. He wished he had put on one of the hunting jackets in the cave. How Davis sat out here in his sweatshirt, he didn't know. Too late now, he thought as he reached up to grab a branch and pull himself into the tree. It took a few minutes for his eyes to adjust to the darkness, but the moonlight helped a little. He slowly moved up the tree to the big fork. Standing as tall as he could, he looked out toward the town. He could make out the lights on the highway as it wound by the high school and past the fire station. He squinted and saw the faintest glow in the direction of the main street. His hope grew slightly, but he saw no cars moving down what was usually a bustling highway for oil and livestock.

There was not enough evidence to make him want to take a closer look. It was frustrating to be so isolated. He was ready to turn on the radio and find out what was happening. Cade fought the deep sadness rising in his throat. Thoughts of his mother hovered around his consciousness, threatening to drag him down into despair. Without trying, he kept imagining her in their house. Alone. Maybe even dead.

He sucked in his breath as if ice water had been thrown in his face. He couldn't take those kinds of thoughts right now. He couldn't think like that and stay strong because he wasn't strong. He wasn't stereotypically tough, either. He loathed football, and he cried at the sad parts in movies. He wasn't his brother, Dylan. He tried to be, but he just wasn't. Even Davis was emotionally stronger than him, he thought. Cade sat in the tree and gazed at the clouds gathering over the moon. What were they going to do when it got colder? At some point, they would have to find better shelter. They could cross-country and get to Austin or San Antonio in a week or two, even with the girls in tow. Maybe they would come across another town that was still okay. Maybe everyone was okay, and people were doing what they were doing - hiding. They'd never know if they didn't try.

Cade leaned back in the tree and decided to take the whole night's watch. Tara would complain tomorrow, but it made him feel tougher. He shoved his hands deep into his sweatshirt pockets and settled in for the rest of the night.

CHAPTER 7

Real Talk

THE HORIZON WAS GLOWING faintly when Cade slowly climbed out of the tree. His back was stiff, and his right leg had fallen asleep, but he had seen the night pass quietly. He shuffled to the cave, picking up branches and twigs for the fire. Ducking inside, his gaze wandered across Davis's and the girls' sleeping forms.

It was chilly and drafty inside, so he knelt and added the wood to the fire. He pulled a lighter from his pocket to start a wad of shredded bark. Once it caught, he shoved it under the fresh firewood. The flames began to lick up at the oak branches, and the fire grew. Cade could feel the cave begin to warm up almost immediately.

Tara stirred on her bedroll, then sat up, startled. She looked around, disoriented, until she saw Cade.

Rubbing her eyes groggily, she asked, "My watch?"

"No, I did it. It's almost morning," Cade whispered.

She dropped her hands to the blanket and then rubbed her legs briskly.

"It's cold!" she said, shivering.

Cade threw another branch on the fire.

"Give it a minute."

Tara reached over and pulled one of his father's old hunting jackets off the pile of blankets and clothes piled together and shoved her arms into the sleeves. She wrapped herself in the camouflage coat and sat there staring at the fire.

Cade stood up, grabbed three more blankets from the pile, and, one by one, placed them over the sleeping children. After he was finished, he came and sat down next to Tara.

"You know, we should just leave. We shouldn't wait."

Tara rubbed her temples and sighed. Then she made the pinchy face Cade knew all too well.

"I can't leave."

"Why?"

"Cade, at least you know something about your mom. I don't even know where my mother is. And the girls," she gestured to the two small forms huddled under the blankets. "Their parents don't even know where they are! We can't just start walking across Texas with someone's kids!"

Tara's voice raised as she spoke, and it was loud enough to wake Davis and the girls. They stirred under the blankets and began to sit up, their hair a tangled mess. The firelight and their sleepy demeanor reminded Cade of Christmas morning, albeit a strange and melancholy one. Tara started rummaging through the plastic bins for something to give everyone for breakfast, muttering to herself. She turned back with some squished honeybuns and juice boxes. After she passed them out to the kids, she grabbed the rifle and went outside. Cade followed.

She dusted her hands on her jeans. Just outside, she turned and leaned against the wall, sliding down to sit. Tara laid the rifle beside her and pulled her knees to her chest, wrapping her arms around her knees. "What if we get somewhere and find out everyone is sick there, too?"

Cade reached around Tara and grabbed the rifle. He checked the chamber.

"You do realize this isn't loaded?"

She grinned at him. "Makes me look tough, though, doesn't it?"

He laughed for the first time in days. Shifting, he reached into one of his cargo pants pockets and pulled out a round. "Want it?"

"Nah," she waved him off. "Unless a cow decides to go carnivore, I don't think I would have anything to shoot at."

"Rattlesnake?"

"I would be running, not shooting."

"Tara, there's plenty to be on the lookout for. First of all, we don't know what's happening to the people who got infected. Then there are coyotes, wild dogs, javelina - seriously! Haven't you lived here all your life?" Cade looked at her like she was losing her mind.

"Yes, but I did my best to stay inside, remember?"

"Yeah, that's true." He turned to face her. "Do you even know how to shoot?"

She shrugged.

"Do you?" he insisted.

"Not technically, but it can't be that hard. I was a top-ranked shooter on MechWorld Attack, legendary level."

This time Cade couldn't control himself. He burst out laughing, eventually laying over on the ground, clutching his side. "You mean," he gasped, "this whole time, all these years, after all, that talk we did about target practice and ammunition storage, you've never actually fired a gun?"

"Not one based in reality."

The two of them laughed for a while. It was therapeutic, Cade thought. After the last few days, they needed a release. The sun was entirely up when they both stood and headed back inside. To their surprise, Davis and the girls had prepared more for breakfast. Five small juice boxes were laid out around the smoldering fire, along with packages of fruit snacks and five small bags of roasted peanuts.

"We figured that the juice boxes said "added cal-
cium" so they could count for dairy, and the fruit
snacks and peanuts cover us for protein and the fruits
and veggies." Allison clasped her hands together and
looked at Tara and Cade proudly. Tara smiled and
ruffled the younger girl's hair.

"Good job. That's using your noggin!"

After breakfast, everyone was burning off pent-up
energy by gathering wood. Tara ducked inside the
shelter momentarily, then returned with something
in her coat. She walked past Cade.

"Cade, come on. Follow me." Tara started to duck
beneath the vines.

"Whoa! Where are you going?"

"Just down the path a bit." She held up the radio she
had hidden in the coat. "So the kids won't hear if it's
bad."

CHAPTER 8

Operation Information

CADE WATCHED TARA GO through the vines. After a glance back, he followed her. They only went a few yards down the trail, but the brush and elevation change would be thick enough to muffle the radio noise. She sat down criss-cross and settled the radio in her lap. Cade couldn't bring himself to get comfortable. Instead, he leaned against a scrubby tree and folded his arms across his chest. Tara clicked on the radio, and they both held their breath.

Nothing.

She looked up at him.

"Change the channel," he said quietly.

She began to sweep the dial up and down, but they only heard static.

"Go to FM."

She switched to the FM band, and they both jumped as they heard loud rap music. She quickly turned down the volume knob. The song ended, and a voice came on. Cade and Tara leaned in to listen.

"Need a new car? Well, today's your lucky day! Come on down to Lucky Automotive for a -"

Tara changed the channel only to hear more of the same.

"They're on auto-pilot," she murmured.

For fifteen minutes, they sat and slowly rolled through all the channels on both the AM and FM channels. They heard nothing but a few stations running on auto and loads of static.

"Don't we have a weather radio?"

Cade furrowed his brows.

"Why on earth would they issue weather updates when no one is reporting the news?"

"You 'tard. The weather broadcast band is one of those no-frills things. Strictly info. It even sounds bad - like the state park weather condition radio things. You remember the signs on the highway that say, for current road conditions, tune to ... whatever you tune to. We used to try all the time and could never hear anything except a really bad signal."

Cade slowly nodded.

"Maybe we're too far. We barely get cell signal, much less crappy radio signals."

Tara had picked up the radio and tucked it back inside her coat. She was walking around purposefully toward the vines and the oak. Sunlight was warming the area. She reached up to the same branch Cade had pulled himself up with the night before and swung her legs up and over with a grunt. Scrambling, she began to scale the thick, wide branches past the fork up into the higher branches.

"Be careful! I don't know how to set a broken leg!" Cade called up, half joking, half serious.

Davis and the girls slowly emerged from the cave entrance, sipping on their juice boxes. They watched intently as Tara found a perch higher than any of them dared to go. She held onto a branch with one hand and pulled out the radio with the other. Holding it to her teeth, she bit down on the switch and jerked to turn it on. She was so high up that no one on the ground could hear if any sound was coming from the speakers.

"What is she doing?"

Davis had come to stand beside his brother. He squinted up into the tree.

"Trying to get a radio signal."

"Which radio is she using?"

"The only one we have." Cade looked down at his brother.

"We could get Dad's old CB. I know where it is."

"So do I. In his truck that isn't at the house."

Davis shook his head.

"Bud, what are you talking about?"

Davis shielded his eyes with one hand. He kept watching Tara.

"She's gonna fall."

"Davis. What CB are you talking about?"

"The one I set up in my fort last year." Davis gave a hint of a smile.

Cade looked back up at Tara.

"Anything?"

"Hold on," she hollered back down.

She made the slow climb back down the tree. When she finally dropped from the last branch, her face showed little indication of what she might have heard, so Cade ventured a guess.

"Nothing?"

She shook her head.

"No, I got something, but I couldn't understand it. It was in Spanish. The lady sounded upset and scared. I could only understand a few words like 'lo siento' and 'familia' and 'mal'."

She looked around at everyone and said, "No one here just happens to speak Spanish?"

Four blank faces stared back at her.

"No, I figured."

"Davis says he knows where a CB is that's safe to get to."

Tara's face brightened.

"I'll go. You guys stay here." Cade turned toward the trail.

"Oh no, you don't. Not by yourself. And I am not staying here with the kids." She went into the cave and grabbed the 22. On her way back out, she added, "Like a babysitter."

"Want bullets this time?" Cade was grinning.

Ignoring him, she turned to Davis and the girls.

"Do not leave this area. Do not take your eyes off each other." She paused a moment, letting her words hang in the air. Davis saluted her and sat down where he had been standing.

"I won't move from this spot."

Cade pulled back the vines to leave but called out over his shoulder to Davis, "I am leaving the pellet gun. It's inside. Don't "not move" until you go get it."

Davis was scrambling into the shelter before Cade could even turn around to leave.

CHAPTER 9

Mission #1

THE TREK FROM THE shelter, down the trail, and up the road was longer than Cade thought. Perhaps it was the anxiety of not knowing what to expect. Mom hadn't come to get them, Dad hadn't magically appeared, and they couldn't hear anything that made sense on the radio. He thought he might have heard some automotive noises a day or two ago, but where their shelter was located, sounds carried in strange ways.

Slowly and silently, Cade and Tara picked their way down the trail. Twenty minutes saw them to the gravel road past the creek, and another twenty got them within shooting distance of the house. When the house was more than just a blur in the distance, Cade broke off through the pasture to the right. He held the barbed wire apart for Tara to slide through, then she did the same for him. They continued to walk in silence.

The sun was up to about three-quarters till noon, and the temperature had risen enough to make tiny sweat beads form on their foreheads. They trekked through the waist-high coastal grass that turned from soft green to gold. Ten more minutes, and they reached the spot where the creek curled up clos-est to the house. Davis had created his fort here among the cedar and mesquite trees. He had ferreted away old fence posts and scrap lumber and had con-structed an elaborate maze of passages and miniature rooms. Cade and Tara ducked into the opening on the side facing away from the creek, mindful of the dirt-dauber and yellow jacket nests.

Inside, the fort was littered with old hunting mag-azines, a couple of Avengers comics, and, oddly enough, a recycle bin filled with juice boxes and soda cans. Cade chuckled at Davis' sense of civility. It was a homemade fort in the South Texas country, but by God, it was a green one!

"Davis did this himself?" Tara asked.

"I think so."

Why didn't I ever see it? I practically live here."

"He liked to be secretive. I don't think Dad ever knew about it either."

They crawled to the biggest room and saw the CB radio on a milk crate. It had been draped with an old clear plastic dry-cleaning bag. It was the old battery-operated model their dad used when he went out on horseback. Since they had stopped running cattle during of the draught, it had been retired to the garage until Davis resurrected it. Cade's only concern was -

"What about batteries?" Tara was already lifting the plastic.

Cade started to rummage through the three old Styrofoam ice chests next to the crate.

"I figured he had some out here, but we have a bunch back at the shelter."

Tara cocked her head to the side.

"We have 9 volt?"

Cade thought hard. "I don't remember. Hey - you're the supply expert. Do we?"

Tara shook her head.

"It was on my 'Dummy you forgot that' list, but I hadn't checked it off yet."

Cade helped Tara untangle the cords and wrap them up neatly so they would fit in his backpack. After they had stowed it away, Cade took a breath and said, "I know where some are, but we'd have to go down to the barn."

Tara nodded grimly.

"We don't have a choice."

"We can go around the back side behind the horse pens and use the door at the back of the stalls. That way, no one could see us if they were looking." Cade started crawling out under a loose piece of plywood.

Tara followed, and then they both stood and brushed themselves off. Cade returned to the plywood and adjusted it to fit back against the old fence posts snugly - even better than before they had crawled beneath it. It seemed like the right thing to do, keeping this structure Davis had worked so hard on intact. He closed his eyes for a moment and imagined his little brother building the fort - hammering, designing, and hauling all the pieces out to this spot. He was such a great kid, and in this awfulness, Cade wanted something good to remain for him. It was the least he could do.

CHAPTER 10

Abort Mission

CADE AND TARA WALKED one behind the other down the gentle slope that led to the house and animal pens. Cade motioned for Tara to stop while he surveyed the area.

He scanned the barn's backside and pens, looking for movement. The animals milled around the yard, rummaging in his mother's garden for food. He could only see four goats, his dad's gelding, and the old cow they kept as a family pet named Happy. He didn't see the two mares or any of the chickens. The most troublesome absence was his dog, Bast. He silently prayed that Mom had Bast in the house for protection.

He motioned for Tara to stay put. He carefully trotted down the little hill to the barn's back door and slipped inside.

The barn was musty and dark. He didn't smell any animal smells, which was a good sign; no one had gotten trapped inside without water, so all the livestock at least had a chance at survival. His father's workbench was on the wall in the middle of the stalls. The red metal rolling toolbox was under the bench, so Cade rolled it out and clicked the combination into place. He opened the top of the toolbox and lifted out the plastic box his father kept the 9 volts in. It was heavy - a good sign. He opened the lid to check and was relieved to see several unopened packages. He pulled his backpack off, slid the batteries into his pack, and slung it over his shoulder.

Cade left the barn and waved for Tara to follow him. He headed around the side of the barn back out to the pasture, trying to create a wide path that would take them far from the front of the house and back to the brush line. She was about a hundred yards away when Cade heard crashing in the brush and a loud snort. He froze.

Turning, he saw a large Brahma bull staring at him eye to eye. He was ear-tagged and belonged to someone in the area, but he was clearly out of his own pasture. Cade began to back away, hoping Tara was paying enough attention to notice what was happening. The bull took a step toward him, but Cade held his ground. Slowly, without taking his eyes off the animal, he sidestepped toward the barbed-wire fence. He was much closer to the house than he wanted, but he had no choice now. The fence was twenty feet away. He could make it if he turned and ran, but it would be close. Maybe the bull was putting on a show. Probably not, but one could hope.

Out of the corner of his eye, he could see Tara, who had caught on to what was happening and climbed up a low live oak. She waved her arms at Cade to be sure he saw her; then, she started yelling and shaking the tree. It was enough to turn the bull's head. Cade took his opportunity to turn, duck his head, and run. The fence came closer, and he was there, weaving through the barbed wire not so carefully. In his haste, he misstepped and fell face-first onto the gravel road that led to the house.

He lay there for a few minutes, caught his breath, then laughed aloud. Still lying on the road, he watched the bull trot away toward the far end of the pasture. Moments later, Tara ran through the grass and ducked under the fence.

Cade pushed himself up to his knees and dusted his hands on his jeans. Tara stood in front of him and held her hand out to pull him up. He grasped it and hoisted himself to stand.

"Well, that was fun!"

Tara laughed nervously.

"I got a ton of batteries. Dad had a good stash."

Tara peered over his shoulder at his backpack.

"Did you see anything else in there useful?"

"Honestly, I didn't even look."

Tara rolled her eyes and groaned.

Cade raised his arms and shrugged his shoulders.

"Sorry! I guess I was distracted!"

It was then he turned to look toward the house.

Then he saw the bright orange X spray painted on the door.

Then his heart felt like it would burst out of his chest.

The world spun as adrenaline pumped through his body. He bolted to the house - to his mother - in a dead run without even stopping to breathe.

CHAPTER 11

Redirect and Regroup

CADE'S BREATH CAME HARD and fast, tearing at his lungs like knives. He pumped his legs up the long, winding road with all his strength. The pecan trees lining the drive had dropped their bounty, and the brittle shell pecans scattered as he charged through. He could see the gate coming closer and closer. He grunted with the strain as he sprinted the last few yards to his family's home. Just as he bounded over the metal cattle guard, he heard her scream.

"Cade! No!"

Tara's voice cut through the raw emotion pouring through his brain. It was enough for him to skid to a halt, reality crashing back. As much as he felt he had to charge through the door, he knew he couldn't. The battle of the century raged inside his heart as he yearned to run to his mother's rescue. She was just inside the door. She was probably on the couch, smelling like gardenias and fresh bread. She needed him, and he couldn't dare go near. A primal sound welled in his belly as he sobbed and fell to the ground, clutching at the gravel with his fists.

After a few minutes, his head cleared enough to breathe normally. He heard the soft crunching of gravel behind him, and then Tara was there, sliding her arm around his trembling shoulders. With gentle pressure, she guided him to stand, mindful of blocking his view of the house as she turned him away toward the road. Together, they walked and stumbled back down the road to the creek, where they stopped momentarily.

"I would have done the same thing."

Tara was looking at him; deep lines of concern furrowed her brow.

"What does it mean?" Cade couldn't get his breath. He was crying. "I can guess, but why –"

"It means we have to do what she said and be safe." Tara was fighting to stay calm for Cade's sake.

Cade had never felt so lost in his life. He had a pain growing in his chest that refused to stop. He ached all over. Panic spread, making it even more difficult to breathe, to think. He fell to the ground, clutching his head, and wept. He was sure the orange X meant his mother was gone. What would he tell Davis? Another wave of anguish washed over him, this time bigger and stronger than before. His little brother didn't deserve this. He was too gentle. Cade couldn't even think about it without feeling sick. He looked up at Tara.

"What do I do now?"

She knelt in front of him and took his hands. Tara looked him in the eye, and with a steady voice, she said, "We go to town like we said we would. We can't give up, and we definitely can't sit here and do nothing."

She gently swept his hair out of his eyes.

"Your mother would want you to make sure we were all safe, and we can't be unless we find out what's going on. That means I have to go to town, and you have to go with me." She moved her hands to his shoulders, gripping them tightly.

"You have to have my back."

Cade took a moment, then nodded as he wiped his nose on the back of his sleeve. He stood, looked around for a moment, then adjusted his backpack. "I'm okay."

Tara gave him an understanding smile, then began walking toward the highway. Cade looked back up the road for a moment, then turned to follow Tara toward town, leaving his heart shattered on the dirt road behind them.

CHAPTER 12

Contact

"Okay. We're all set."

Davis snapped the cover back onto the CB radio's battery case. He turned the box over and blew the dust out of the crevices on the front, then flipped the metal switch while everyone held their breath. The green light flickered on.

"Whoop!" Davis fist-bumped the air.

Cade stood and began to pace. He had yet to tell Davis what he had seen at the house. There were no words he could think of that sounded right, so he kept it to himself and let his brother have his moment. Tara sat next to Davis, keeping her eyes locked on Cade.

"So, how do we do this? Just start on channel one?" Tara asked no one in particular.

"Dad always used eight."

Before anyone could respond, Davis turned the dial to eight, picked up the handset, pressed the button, and began to speak.

"This is D. S. in Westhoff. Does anyone copy?"

As he released the button, he looked up at Cade, who had frozen in place. Davis used Westhoff, which was good. It was close but about seven miles away.

Minutes passed. Davis pressed the button again, "This is DS. Does anyone copy? Anyone?"

His voice developed an urgent tone.

Just as he let the handset fall into his lap, a crackle leaped from the small CB speaker, and all five kids jumped.

"Copy that." The voice was male and broken by the static.

"What the - " Tara grabbed the handset from Davis.

"Where are you?" she demanded into the speaker.

"Repeat?" The voice was growing fainter.

"Wher-" she began, almost angrily. She closed her eyes and took a breath.

"Where. Are. You." she enunciated slowly and loudly.

For a long minute, there was silence. The frogs at the creek continued their sawing noise as the kids all waited for an answer.

"Near - Can- La- <static> -ding to San An- o <static>"

"San Antonio? Did you say San Antonio?" Tara was almost shouting into the handset, gripping it so hard her knuckles were white, and her hand shook.

"Is everything ok? Is everyone sick? What should we do?"

Cade grabbed Tara's hand and pried the handset away. She covered her face and began to cry. Long sobs and a high-pitched keening that tore at his heart. Tara, her tough-girl persona gone, was just a girl, and she was scared. Even though he was hurting more than he could bear, he leaned over and pulled her close. He held her as tight as he could, saying nothing. The radio crackled and hissed, but no more of the voice could be heard.

"-hind a hill. You still out there, DS?"

Cade's heart leaped. He snatched up the handset and pressed the button.

"Here! We- I'm here."

"What's the situation in your neck of the woods?" The voice was clearer now. He sounded like an older man, perhaps in his fifties or sixties.

"We don't know. What's going on in San Antonio?"

There was silence. Then the static started again, and the man's voice cut through.

"It's not pretty. Are the people all right out where you are?"

Cade looked up at the rest of the group. Tara shook her head back and forth quickly.

"Not too sure about the local situation," Cade was trying to make himself sound older than he was. He continued, "But we're all right where we are."

The static was lessening.

"Get yourselves away from everyone if you can. The bastards crop-dusted all the major cities with their little buggies. Makes people crazy at first, then real, real mean. Then it makes them dead."

Buggies? A virus? Tara was staring at Cade, her eyes wide with surprise. Almost imperceptibly, she mouthed the word "zombies." Cade shook his head in disbelief.

"What are the symptoms?" Davis whispered in Cade's ear. Cade nodded and pressed that button again to speak.

"How long does it take - once you've been infected?"

There was a long pause, and Cade's heart began to sink.

"Oh....depends. Most people are dropping in about 36 hours. Some take longer - and those are the ones you need to watch out for. They get more than mean."

The voice was beginning to cut in and out again.

"Listen," the man's voice said, "I can tell you're young'uns. Wherever you are, if you can, start making your way to San Antonio. Word has it the army's put a call out to anyone still clear to head to Randolph Air Force Base on the north east side of town. They've set themselves up to take people in and send them to the clean zones once they've been checked."

The kids could hear the sound of wind and the faint rumble of an engine in the background. Whoever they were talking to must be driving. Cade could see the hope that flared up in Davis and Tara's faces.

"Be safe, and don't go near anyone. I'd say I could come get you, but I have just enough gas to get there, and I ain't stopping anywhere to refuel." He chuckled. "Hell, I don't even know if there's any fuel left anyway, with everybody trying to bug out."

Cade's heart sank.

"Thanks. We'll be ok on our own." Cade sat back on his heels and hung his head. The radio crackled again.

"Take care, son. Maybe I'll see you at Randolph. Call out on this channel if you have trouble. I can't get to you, but maybe I can help somehow."

"Thanks. See you...maybe."

CHAPTER 13

The Best Laid Plans

CADE SAT ON THE ground hard and dropped the handset to the dirt. Tara sprung up and paced around the clearing, mumbling to herself. Davis reached over to scan more channels. Cade reached out and grabbed his hand.

"No. There's no use. We got what we needed."

"What? That people are dying, and we must go an impossible distance to a deadly virus-infested city?" Tara snapped.

"It's not impossible."

"Cade! Seriously? It's almost seventy miles away." She was pacing faster now. She reminded Cade of a caged tiger. "What about the girls?"

Allison, who had been sitting near the cave entrance with her sister, stood.

"Bri and I aren't weak. We can keep up with you. But before we leave," she hesitated until her sister stood beside her and took her hand, "we want to leave a note at our house. For our mom."

Cade breathed deeply. He scrambled to his feet and surveyed the others. Davis was still sitting by the CB, his hand on the knobs. Tara was pacing around, and Bri and Allison stood together, their hands gripping one another, faces set in hesitant determination. What was he supposed to do? He wasn't a leader. He never led anything in his life. Tara was better suited to that role, but she was lost in some frantic preoccupation with the dangers the mysterious radio man had alluded to. As she moved near him, he grasped her by the arm. She spun around to face him, a mixture of anger and fear in her expression.

"Do you still want to go into town?" he asked.

"Yes."

"Okay, then." Cade glanced at Davis. "Go up to the pasture and gather some mesquite for the fire. Remember, we cut a bunch of limbs over the summer but never got a chance to put them in the burn pile because it was so dry? They should still be there. Grab as much as you can carry."

Cade guided Tara outside.

"When Davis returns with enough wood to keep the fire going, we'll go. Get a small pack together."

"Enough for two people, right?" She pursed her lips and raised an eyebrow.

"Yes, for two."

As Tara ducked back inside, Davis exited with a large, empty duffle bag slung over his shoulder. He rounded the shelter and started up the slope towards the pasture. Just as the top of his head disappeared, Cade called out to his brother.

"Be careful!"

Cade's little brother lifted his hand and waved, and then he was gone.

***

Davis walked along the cattle trail winding through the scrubby oaks and mesquite, carefully watching his step. He had been trained at an early age to be aware of the ground around him because rattlesnakes and copperheads called the area home. It was nearly November, so the cooler air slowed snakes down, but he knew surprising one was never a good idea. Out here, it could be deadly.

He had nearly filled the canvas duffle bag with small branches and was considering turning back when he heard it - the most unexpected human noise. It was a car trying to start. The chugging, repeated whirring of the engine trying to turn over startled him, and he nearly forgot to breathe. He was close to the highway, so he dropped his bag and crept through a stand of mesquite toward the fence. His heart hammered in his chest. Sunlight glinted off the metallic blue of the car body, so Davis tried squinting through the branches to see better. He detected movement but couldn't tell who or what it was.

Finally, he reached a spot where he could see the whole car. It looked like a new, small sedan. The hood wasn't open, but the driver's side door was. A woman with red hair was inside, slumped over the steering wheel. She was rocking slightly back and forth, and then it became apparent she was crying. Davis' first instinct was to run over and see if she was hurt, but he caught himself. He debated whether or not he should do anything or go tell Cade and Tara. He knew Cade would be furious if he made a big decision like that without him, so he stood, turning back toward his bag and the cattle trail. He would return to the shelter and let his brother make the call.

Before he could take a step, a blinding pain shot up his leg. He yelped and fell backward, crashing into the brush. He hit the ground and watched a rattlesnake's tail disappear into the scrub. The realization hit him, and he began to panic – a rattlesnake. He pulled the leg of his jeans up to reveal two small puncture wounds just above his left ankle. Before getting a good look at his wound, he heard the crunching and snapping sounds of someone making their way through the brush, coming in his direction.

"Hello?" It was a female voice.

Davis could barely breathe. Through gritted teeth, he grunted, "Here!"

Seconds later, a teenage girl emerged through the trees; twigs and leaves stuck in her long, red ponytail. She looked frightened, but her expression changed to worry when she saw Davis lying on the ground in obvious pain.

"What happened?" she scanned him for apparent injury.

"Snakebite. Rattlesnake."

CHAPTER 14

Tick Tock

DAVIS FELT CLAMMY AND nauseous. He pulled his jeans leg higher and pointed to the puncture wounds. The area around his ankle was beginning to swell.

The redheaded girl knelt beside him and examined his leg closely. "Are you positive it was a rattlesnake?"

Davis nodded. Breathing was getting harder, so he didn't feel like speaking. Sweat was beading up on his forehead.

"Ok. We need to get you somewhere safe." She looked over her shoulder back toward the road. "How old are you?"

"Ten." He grunted, squeezing his eyes closed.

"I can get you to my car, and you can lie in the back seat. My dad's clinic is pretty close. I can bring antivenin if I can get there and back in time. He always had some in case a rancher got bit."

She began to position herself to pick Davis up, but Davis squirmed away.

"Wait a minute!" he pushed her back. "Who are you?"

"Kennedy Sample. I'm Dr. Sample's daughter."

Davis shook his head. "I didn't know he had a daughter."

"I live with my mom in Austin." She worked her arms under his knees and around his back. With a grunt, she lifted Davis and began to push back through the brush. They continued silently; the only sound was her labored breathing and dry grass crunching beneath her feet. As they neared the barbed wire fence, she shook Davis gently.

"Hey, you still with me?" She nudged his head with her chin.

Davis nodded.

"I'm gonna set you down, and I want you to crawl under the wire while I hold it." She gently lowered him to stand on his good leg. Kennedy stepped on the lowest wire with one foot and pulled up on the next highest. She motioned with her head to Davis.

He ducked under the wire, crying out in pain when he put weight on his left foot. Kennedy followed, and before he knew it, she had scooped him back up and was heading for her car. But before they crossed the road, Davis looked up at her.

"Davis. My name is Davis Miller."

She smiled.

"You're gonna be ok, kiddo," she said reassuringly.

She set him down again, this time beside the small blue car. He leaned on the back end while she opened the back door and rearranged the bags, then she stood and brushed her hands on the back of her jeans.

"Ok. Let's get you in and take another look at that leg."

"Wait. We need to get my brother and Tara. They are probably back at camp by now."

"Camp?" she shook her head. "There's no time. It'll be useless if I don't get that antivenin in you within the next four hours. Now, come on. It's gonna take me at least an hour to get to my dad's on foot."

"Why can't you drive?"

"Car's out of gas."

"If," Davis winced as she adjusted his leg, "-we get Cade, he can get some from our barn." Davis was shaking and getting paler. "It's only about twenty minutes away."

She looked at Davis hard. "There is no way you can walk."

"I can tell you how to get there."

The sweat was running down his face but he continued, his voice weak and shaky.

"Take my bag so he knows you are telling the truth. I left it where you found me."

She looked at the sky, then down the road.

"Only twenty minutes?"

Davis nodded.

She reached inside and grabbed her backpack and a bottle of water. She leaned in and handed it to Davis.

"Drink all of this. It had better be gone when I get back, ok? Now," she slung her backpack over her shoulder. "Now, how do I get there?"

CHAPTER 15

Time is of the Essence

KENNEDY DUCKED UNDER THE fence, trying to appear confident as she returned to the brush. The boy, Davis, was in real danger, but the odds would be much better if he were right about his brother being able to get gas for her car. She saw his bag lying on the ground ahead of her. It was full of broken limbs and sticks. She shook the contents onto the ground to make it easier for her to carry and slung it over her shoulder. She ducked through a heavy brush stand and emerged in the open along the edge of a pasture.

The boys' directions were simple. Follow the pasture to where the land begins to drop off. There would be a trail between two big rocks, and it would lead her to the shelter. She took a deep breath and broke into a jog. In minutes, she found the trail nestled between the two big rocks, just as Davis said. Then, scattering rocks and dust, she descended the steep slope. The trail flattened out, and she slowed, not wanting to burst into a situation unannounced. She could hear voices calling out.

"Davis!"

It was a boy.

She hesitated. Then, another voice, this time female, sounded.

"Davis! Where are you?"

Kennedy breathed deeply and then raised her voice.

"Hello?" she shouted.

There was a brief hesitation, then the sound of running and crashing. Seconds later, a boy – Cade, most likely – exploded out of the trees right. She jumped back, stumbling on the rocks. A girl followed, heading straight for Kennedy. The girl grabbed Kennedy roughly by the shoulders, shaking her and shouting.

"Where is he? What did you do?"

Cade pulled his friend back.

"Tara!" he barked. "Stop!"

Kennedy took a few steps forward. "It's okay," she said. "I'd do the same thing, too." She reached for the bag slung over her shoulder.

"We don't have much time. You're Cade, right?"

He nodded.

"Your brother is back at the highway. He's in my car. He's got a rattlesnake bite on his leg, and I need gas to get to my dad's clinic and find antivenin."

She looked at Cade and Tara.

"We have about three hours before the antivenin isn't any help."

For a moment, Cade simply stood and stared.

"We have *three hours*," Kennedy repeated.

"Who are you?" Tara insisted.

"Kennedy Sample."

"Dr. Sample's daughter? I thought you lived in Houston."

Kennedy unslung Davis' bag and handed it to Cade. "Austin, actually."

Cade, who had been silent, reached out and grabbed the bag. "If you say we have three hours, then we need to go now." He turned to Tara. "You should go find her car and stay with Davis."

Tara nodded and started to push past Kennedy to head up the trail.

"Wait!" Kennedy called.

She turned.

"If you have more water, take it. And any medical supplies you have, just in case .... there are problems."

Tara shot a look of fear at Cade, then nodded at Kennedy as she darted back through the brush in the direction they came from. Cade motioned to Kennedy as he ducked back into the brush. She followed him through to the clearing where their shelter was situated. Tara had just disappeared inside.

"How far do we have to go?" Kennedy asked as Cade continued through the clearing to another trailhead.

"Not far – maybe fifteen minutes," he said to her without looking back.

"I didn't tell your friend where my car was," Kennedy said with concern. Cade glanced back at her.

"She'll find it. There's only one highway, and it's pretty straight." He turned back toward the trail and picked up his speed. Kennedy had no choice but to push harder and follow.

Ten minutes later, the barn came into view. Cade looked back over his shoulder at Kennedy. She hadn't said a word since they left the clearing by the shelter. He broke off to the right, ducked through the barbed wire fence, and Kennedy followed. As they approached the barn, he slowed and motioned for her to stop. He crept forward, then turned his head. "Get low, " he mouthed, gesturing at the same time.

She crouched down and checked her watch. The trek had taken fifteen minutes, as he said. She looked up, as he disappeared around the side of the barn. The sun was out but still chilly, made worse by the wind, which was picking up. She scanned the sky and noticed the clouds were thickening along the western horizon. Kennedy glanced back toward the barn. Cade was already coming around the side, a red gas can in each hand. He jogged in a crouch back to her position, setting one can beside her before he kept going. She picked hers up and followed.

They traveled back to the shelter area in silence; the only sound was their breathing, which had become heavier and more labored. Kennedy struggled to keep up, and by the time they had made the clearing, she dropped her can and sat down hard.

"Wait!" she panted.

Cade turned. His chest was heaving, but he showed no indication that he was ready to stop.

"I need a minute," Kennedy said, putting her head on her knees.

"We don't have a minute," Cade growled.

He turned and headed for the trees and the trail that led up to the pasture. With a groan, Kennedy rose, grabbed her can, and pressed on. She couldn't even see Cade as limbs slapped at her face and scratched her arms, but she pushed on toward the trail. Finally, she burst through the brush onto the barely visible dirt pathway. She saw Cade's dust cloud ahead but she did not see him. He must have reached the top of the slope and was headed down the tree-line. She took a deep breath and doubled her efforts, clearing the top of the hill in a handful of long, bounding strides. Cade was waiting for her a few hundred feet down the trail. She half-jogged to catch up to him.

"Where do we cut across?" He was scanning the brush that separated the pasture from the highway fence.

"Not much further," she said, pointing down to a spot where her bright orange backpack lay.

He nodded and picked up his can. Together, they jogged to the pack and the break in the brush that would lead them to her car and, more importantly, to Davis.

CHAPTER 16

Rescue Mission… Possible?

TARA SCRAMBLED INTO THE shelter, her heart racing. Where was the medical bag? She pushed cartons and boxes aside until she saw the red canvas beneath a pile of blankets. Quickly, she unzipped it and shoved five bottles of water inside.

"Tara?" The girls stood in the opening, gripping each other's hands. "Where is everyone?"

Tara pursed her lips. "Davis is hurt. I'm getting supplies, and we'll bring him back in a few hours. I need you to stay put until we get back."

"We can help." Allison let her sister's hand fall as she stepped forward, squaring her shoulders. "We aren't babies."

Tara clambered to her feet and hefted the bag over her shoulder.

"I know you aren't babies, dummy. But I need you to make up a pallet for Davis and organize the medical supplies." She looked both of the girls in the eye. "Can you do that?"

Brianna nodded. Allison stayed quiet, but with her silence, she agreed.

"Good. Be back soon," Tara called as she darted out the door.

Ducking her head, she barreled through the brush to the trail. She didn't stop until she was over the top of the slope and halfway down the pasture trail. An orange bandana caught her eye – it must have been one of the girl's. Breathing heavily, Tara turned and scrambled through the mesquite scrub, pushing on until she saw the fence through the huisache and sage. A glint of metallic silver and blue glinted through the brush, and she pressed on under the fence that separated the pasture from the highway shoulder.

The car was sitting in the middle of the road as if it had simply stopped in place. All the windows were rolled down, and the back passenger door was slightly open. She sprinted to the car.

"Davis?" She pulled the door open gingerly as if it was Davis himself.

His eyes were closed, and he was propped against the other door on a pile of clothes and blankets, a large, half-empty bottle of water resting against his chest. Despite the cold, he was sweating and looked pale and waxy. At the sound of Tara's voice, he opened his eyes and managed a weak smile.

"Het there," he said quietly, sounding like a weak version of himself.

Tara opened the front driver-side door and climbed inside. She didn't want to disturb his leg but wanted to get closer to him. He turned his head as she leaned through the two front seats to brush his hair off his forehead.

"What do I do?" she whispered to herself.

"That girl. Did she find you?" Davis whispered.

"Yes. She and Cade went for gas so we can drive the car into town and get the medicine for you," Tara said.

"It really hurts," he groaned, then closed his eyes again.

She continued stroking his hair, unsure of what else might help. After a few minutes, she gently shook Davis' shoulder.

"Davis, you need to drink the water," she lifted the bottle from his lap to his lips. He opened his eyes and took the bottle from her. His hands shook as he took a long drink. Tara checked her watch. Though she didn't remember exactly when she left the campsite, she estimated it had been about thirty minutes. Cade and Kennedy should be arriving any minute. She re-flexively looked over to the fence, but a moan from Davis pulled her attention back. He was grimacing in pain.

"Davis?"

Tara's heart was in her throat. Just then, she heard footsteps running across the pavement. Without even looking, she cried out.

"Cade!"

The panic in her voice was unmistakable.

Cade's face appeared in the doorway. Tara could see Kennedy at the car's rear, filling the tank, she assumed. Cade's face was a mask of fear and worry.

"He's in a lot of pain," Tara told him.

Before Cade could respond, Kennedy opened the driver-side door. She turned the ignition, and the car fired to life.

"Hour and a half. Let's go, people!"

Cade slid into the back seat with Davis, mindful of his leg, which was swelling and turning purple. Davis was sweating more, and his color had grayed considerably. Cade reached across the seat and grasped his little brother's hand.

"Don't stop till we get there. I don't care what you have to run over."

CHAPTER 17

It Won't Kill You, But...

THE NEXT FEW MINUTES went by in silence. Kennedy gripped the wheel, grim determination on her face, while Tara constantly went from scanning ahead to turning in the seat to check on Davis. Cade hadn't taken his eyes off of his brother since they started the car. Davis let out an occasional groan but was silent otherwise.

"Make sure he's drinking that water," Kennedy called to the back.

Cade squeezed his brother's hand.

"C'mon buddy, let's have a drink."

Davis opened his eyes and nodded as Cade raised the bottle to his lips. Just then, the car jolted, and Davis coughed and sputtered as he got a face full of water. As his body shuddered with the force of his coughing fit, he cried out in pain. Cade, visibly panicked, barked at Kennedy.

"Be careful!"

Kennedy only gripped the wheel harder as she hit the gas and sped across the bridge leading into town. The clinic was just on the other side, and she could see the red and white marquee – "Gonzales County Family Clinic, Dr. Jefferson Sample, M.D."

They crossed the bridge, and Kennedy made a hard right into the gravel parking lot. She haphazardly pulled up by the front door, threw the transmission into park, and jumped out of the car. She ran around to the doors and pulled, a look of surprise crossing her face as the door opened without hesitation.

"Get him inside, quick!" she called out as she disappeared inside.

Tara looked to Cade. He was already climbing out of the car. He came around to the passenger side.

"Hold him up while I open this door," he called to Tara.

She leaned through the seats and grasped Davis firmly by the shoulders.

"Got him!"

Cade opened the door and scooped his brother up in one smooth motion. Davis whimpered and began to cry. Tara ran to the clinic door and held it for the boys. Once inside, they followed the sounds of cabinets slamming shut and deposited Davis on an examination table in an exam room marked "Trauma." Kennedy had already turned the bright overhead lights on and pulled out a medical instrument tray. As Cade untangled himself from Davis, she ran out of the room.

"Be right back!"

More cabinet slamming could be heard across the hall, and then she was back in the room. She had a small vial in her hand and a disappointed look on her face. She glanced up at Cade and Tara's questioning looks.

"It expired last month, but that's all we have."

She grabbed a syringe and filled it with saline. Her hands shook, so she turned her back, carefully inject- ing a small amount into the vial. Kennedy pulled the needle out and tossed the syringe into the corner.

"Hey!"

Cade glared at her while wiping his brother's fore- head with a paper towel.

"I can't use that one now. I need a clean nee- dle," Kennedy snapped just before she pulled a sterile package from her pocket. Cradling the vial between her pinky and ring finger, she pulled the paper apart, revealing another syringe.

"It's a 12-gauge, but that's all I could find in a hurry."

Tara's eyes widened at the sight of the thick needle.

"We treat cattle and horses! They have thick skin!"

Kennedy bit down on the syringe cap and pulled the needle free before shoving it into the rubber stopper. She shot five cc's of air into the vial and as she released the plunger, the cloudy antivenin solution filled the syringe.

"Pull his jeans down. I need a big muscle." Kennedy crossed the room and made for the side of the exam table by Cade. She gestured to Davis' back pocket. "We usually give snake antivenom in an IV, but unless any of you went to nursing school, this is the best we can do."

Cade nodded and pulled the beltline of his brother's jeans down enough for Kennedy to access the top of Davis' read end. Kennedy pinched the skin.

"Wait!"

Tara grabbed Kennedy's hand.

"This won't, you know, *hurt* him, will it?"

Kennedy glanced at Tara, her mouth set in a grim line.

"This won't, but the snakebite? That'll definitely do it if we don't get this in him now."

CHAPTER 18

We're Gonna Need a Bigger Person

CADE WASN'T SURE WHAT he expected to see after Kennedy depressed the plunger into Davis' hip. Too many late-night movies had him half-expecting his little brother to begin thrashing around and foaming at the mouth. The three of them stood over Davis, barely breathing.

Davis's skin was pale and clammy, sweat on his brow and upper lip.

"What now?" Cade squeezed Davis' hand, his eyes darting back and forth from Kennedy to Tara.

"We wait."

Kennedy turned back to the cluttered countertop, rummaging through the haphazard piles. Cade watched as she tossed empty gauze packages to the side with one hand while she lifted small boxes and packets of syringes with the other, muttering to herself all the while.

"What are you looking for?"

"Ah ha!" Kennedy turned, holding a white bottle in her hand. "This!"

Cade grabbed the bottle and eyed it warily. "PRN Stat?"

Kennedy grabbed it back out of Cade's grasp and twisted the cap. Sharp clicks sounded as she broke the cap's protective seal. She let out a breath. "Whew. It's new. I was hoping for that." She gestured with the bottle. "This needs to be handy over the next few hours. Anti-venin can make people really nauseous. This nutrition gel might be the fastest way to keep his energy up. We use it on the animals here, but I assume it's good enough for people, too."

"How long?" Tara whispered.

Kennedy looked confused.

Tara cleared her throat and spoke more clearly. "How long until we know if he's okay?"

"By morning, most likely."

There was little sound in the room for a handful of minutes, save for Davis' rapid and shallow breaths. Cade found kennel pads and folded a makeshift pillow for his little brother while Kennedy cut the pant leg away from the bite area. Tara stood at Davis' feet, unmoving, staring at the end of the table. Cade looked up as he settled Davis' head on the pads.

"You okay?"

"No," she murmured. "None of us is okay. The girls are by themselves, and Davis is snakebit. This is not okay on any level." She leveled her gaze at Cade. "We're kids. We need adults."

"She's not wrong," Kennedy agreed, looking up from Davis' wounded leg. "An actual doctor would be fantastic right about now."

"I'm going."

Tara turned and started for the door.

"Tara, wait." Cade pushed past the clutter on the floor to follow, catching her arm before she could leave. She pulled her arm away.

"We're in town already, so I might as well do what I set out to do while we're here." She didn't wait for Cade to respond.

"Where is she going?"

Cade turned to see Kennedy, scissors in one hand and gauze in the other. She had pulled her tangled blonde hair back in a haphazard braid, but most of it was coming out. The absurdity of the moment took hold, and Cade let loose a quick breath. Tara was right. They needed help.

"She's going into town." He pointed at his brother. "You got this?"

She nodded.

"Good. Because I'm going with her. Keep doing what you're doing, and we'll be back before the morning."

Kennedy nodded towards a closet door near Cade.

"Dad kept his rifle in there. He used it sometimes when he had to go out looking for livestock to treat. You'll need it."

He nodded and opened the door. As he slung the rifle over his shoulder, he gave her a quick smile of thanks.

"Keep my brother alive," he said in a low voice. "Please."

Cade turned and followed Tara out into the clinic lobby. The sunlight was bright compared to the single fluorescent light in a small treatment room. He squinted.

"You sure about this?"

"As sure as I can be." Tara shook her head and pulled the front door open. "What else are we going to do?"

Cade shrugged. "Stay put? Stay safe?"

She looked over her shoulder, and where Cade expected to see an encouraging smile, he saw his best friend's grim determination. She gestured for him to follow.

"Safe isn't an option anymore."

CHAPTER 19

Into the Unknown

TARA HAD ALREADY POSITIONED herself on the far side of the concrete bridge, binoculars out by the time Cade scrambled up the embankment to join her behind the guardrail. He always thought the bridge at the edge of town was overkill because its long span was over a tiny creek with barely enough water for minnows. But the ravine was steep on one side with a gentle slope on the other. A memory of the year it snowed briefly fluttered through his thoughts. He chuckled, recalling their awkward attempt at sledding down the hill once the thin, crusty layer of snow decided to stick.

He snapped back to the present and pushed on. By the time he reached Tara, he was panting.

"Took you long enough."

She continued to scan the houses just past the school.

"I didn't think you were going to run all the way," he whispered, trying to catch his breath.

"I'm just trying not to waste time. In MechWarrior Assult, the gamers that stayed on the move scored better."

Her attempt at levity pulled a hint of a smile from Cade. The deep shadows that had formed in her expression over the past hour still clung, but he could see she was trying to hide it.

But just as the darkness in her expression receded, it changed back to grim. She stopped scanning with the binoculars and settled her sights on the highway leading into town. Cade followed the direction she was focused on, but he couldn't see movement: no cars, no dogs - nothing.

Several cars were along the roadside, some neatly pulled over and others more haphazardly askew on the pavement. Cade watched as she focused her binoculars on one of the vehicles.

"Crap, " she muttered. Then she cleared her throat and set her jaw as she brought the binoculars down and stuffed them back into her bag. Tara pulled out a smaller set and handed them to Cade. He took them and settled beside her, positioning himself to look through the railings.

"What'd you see?" Cade asked as she pulled her arms through the pack's straps.

"Nothing."

Cade looked at her.

She nodded. "See for yourself."

He lifted the small binoculars and trained his focus on the cars, where he saw a form slumped in the driver's seat. He blew out a breath and sat on the ground, turning to lean against the metal rail.

"Hey," Cade began, "I brought something for you." He set the binoculars to the side, pulled a gas mask from his backpack, and handed it to Tara. She reached for it, but Cade didn't let go.

"I should go with you."

Tara shook her head firmly.

"Think. If we both go, and something happens, what about Davis and the girls?"

"Then I should go, and you should stay here." Cade started to pull out another mask.

"That makes no sense." Tara tightened her pack straps. "I am the one who has lived in town my whole life. I know every backyard fence. I know people's cars - even their dogs. It will be faster and safer if I go."

Cade reluctantly nodded in agreement.

"Ok. But if you aren't back here in thirty minutes, I am coming after you. Got it?"

She nodded and pulled the mask over her head, reaching back to tighten the straps. She stood, stepped over the guardrail, and jogged to the other side of the bridge. Once the pavement sprawled onto solid ground, Tara stepped into the grass and trotted to the line of fences just off the road. Cade watched as she crouched and pulled out the binoculars. Then she rose, sprinted to the end of the fence line, peered around the corner, turned, and gave Cade a thumbs up. In seconds, she disappeared around the corner.

Cade stared at the spot where Tara had just been. He tore his gaze from the corner and began to look at the back of the houses behind the fence. There was no sign of movement, no sign of anything.

He sat back against the guard rail and started the long vigil, waiting for his best friend to return.

CHAPTER 20

You've Trained for This, Right?

TARA COULDN'T DECIDE WHETHER to walk out in the open or try to hide her presence. She felt silly slinking along the hedges and bushes of her own neighborhood, but she knew it was the safest bet.

Everything was quiet. There were no car noises, no children playing, or even barking dogs that she could hear. Looking up at the sky, she noticed no birds flying or flitting through the trees.

Through the mask, her breathing seemed loud, the silence surrounding her making it all the more strange. She couldn't help but feel like she was in a movie. As she passed the front of the first house, an orange X revealed itself, painted across the front door. Tara sucked in her breath as the memory of Cade running to his own house came crashing back. She scanned all the doors on both sides of the street.

Most were the same - picturesque small-town houses scarred with the orange X which she was positive didn't mean anything good.

She kept going.

House after house, it was the same - no signs of people, alive or dead. It felt as if everyone on the street had disappeared. But as she was settling into the idea that she would not encounter anything unpleasant, she noticed something on the front porch of the big yellow house on the corner. As she moved closer, she could see clothes. Finally, it became apparent when she stood directly in front of the house. It was Mr. Belton sitting on his porch swing, slumped over to the side.

She almost ran to the porch to help him, but the buzzing of flies stopped her. They were busily hovering around Mr. Belton's still form, and she took it as a sign that she could not help him now.

She squeezed her eyes shut and held her breath, waiting for the wave of fear and sadness to wash over her, but it only lapped quietly at her feet. Tara moved on, clinging to her grim determination while she walked along the bushes instead of crouching. There was no time for stealth and, apparently, no need.

Fewer cars were lining the street than usual. It seemed like many were gone. Maybe everyone left, she thought. There were a few here and there, and inside one or two homes were shapes of people slumped over to one side. Her heart ached, hoping not to recognize anyone. Eventually, she found herself staring at the pavement as she walked.

She turned down Hackberry Street, heading for her own house, when she heard the first noise - a hacking cough from a parked car on the opposite side of the street. The cough came again, this time accompanied by a low, guttural growl. She crouched instinctively and froze as she heard a raspy voice.

"Smythe!"

Tara looked in the direction of the car. Her heart leaped. Coach Garza was leaning back in the driver's seat of his navy blue SUV, coughing and shaking. She began running in his direction when he turned toward her.

"NO!" he barked. He covered his face with one arm and held out the other to motion for her to stop. "Get back!"

Tara slowed down but didn't stop completely.

"Tara Smythe, you stop right now!" he began to growl and grab at the car's door frame. One minute, he was clawing at the door like a rabid dog trying to get out, and then he threw himself back against the seat in an apparent struggle, *but with whom?* He was groaning and growling, covered in sweat.

He was so pale. He struggled as he breathed in. His violently trembling hands and clenched the steering wheel as he stared forward, not making eye contact.

"You gotta go."

"But coach," she kept walking forward, her heart racing.

"Listen to me!" he shouted, eyes still fixed on the front of the truck.

She stopped and held her breath.

"It's bad. If you aren't sick, then go. Nobody here is left." He clenched his teeth and grimaced, turning and staring directly at her, his bloodshot, puffy eyes boring into her. "I mean nobody."

Tara glanced past the truck to see her house. The front door was ajar, and her mother's car was haphazardly parked in the driveway.

"And if anyone here were still alive, like me, you don't.... want....... to be around." He released a deep, primal scream and clawed at his face with both hands.

"Go! Go! GO!"

CHAPTER 21

What Now?

TARA SPUN AROUND, RUNNING as hard as she could. She stopped at the corner, heaving breaths intertwined with sobs. It was all unbelievably true. She couldn't fight the images of her mother, sick like Coach. She felt like she was suffocating, so she ripped the mask off. She was still crying, tears streaming down her face, and she squeezed her eyes closed. She could hear him still screaming as she took off in another sprint back towards the bridge. As she made the last corner, she almost ran Cade over.

Cade righted himself and grabbed her by the shoulders to keep her from falling backward. He was worriedly looking her over.

"Tara! I heard you scream! What happened? Are you all right?"

"It...." she breathed hard, "wasn't me."

Tara wiped her eyes on her sleeves, grabbed Cade's hand, and began to run for the bridge, pulling Cade behind her. He stumbled, dropping her hand, but regained his speed to catch up just as she leaped over the bridge railing. She fell to the ground but scrambled to push herself to sit beneath the concrete wall. Breathing hard, she turned to Cade when he collapsed beside her. He flipped around to stare at Tara. She seemed dazed; tear stains streaked her dirty face.

"Cade," she was staring out at nothing. "I saw Coach. He was still alive."

Cade's heart pounded. Alive?

"But he was sick. He wouldn't let me get close. He told me to leave and not to come back, that it would be really bad if we got sick." She looked at Cade, the threatening tears now rolling down her cheeks. "His car was parked outside my house. Mom's car was there, but he told me to leave." She searched Cade's face. "He said I should *leave!*"

She started to sob. Cade leaned over and pulled her to him. He knew that Coach Garza and Tara's mother had been dating for a while and that if he was telling Tara to leave without seeing her mom, it could only mean one thing.

The weight on Cade's shoulders settled in, heavier than he thought he could bear. His thoughts went to Davis and what they might find when they returned to the clinic, and his heart seized, clenched with a fist of fear. If he lost Davis, he might as well die, too. Tara and the girls were the only thing that would keep him from waking into town and being done with everything.

Cade gripped the back of Tara's head with one hand and pressed his cheek against her hair. Even through the dirt and sweat, he could still smell a hint of her strawberry Power Puff girls shampoo - the one he teased her mercilessly about.

"She's gone, isn't she?" Tara's voice was barely a whisper against his shoulder.

"Tara, I-"

Her sobs faded to whimpers, then she sniffled a few times before she went still. She sat back and took a few deep breaths, staring at him momentarily. Her reddish hair was still twisted up in a messy knot and though she wore no make-up, the tears streaked through the dust and smudges of grime on her face. Her grey tank top and jeans were standard Tara - the 22 caliber rifle slung across her back was the only difference. She narrowed her eyes and looked hard at Cade.

"I suppose I knew the answer to that before I went in. They're all dead. And if they aren't, they will be before long." She pulled Allison's note to her mother out of her pocket and crumpled it in her hand. Standing up, she let it fall to the ground.

"There's nothing left. We have to leave. Now."

Acknowledgements

I would like to thank Imagine Dragons for their "Radioactive" video. For whatever reason, the story, the images, and the music sparked this idea.

About the Author

Tabitha Leigh is obsessed with all the fantastical tales that make life interesting. She believes in fairies, elves, magic, and that good always conquers evil.

***

More from Tabitha Leigh and others authors at
www.thebookishberg.com